Love Audrina.
x

DRIVE BY

An Electric Eclectic Book

By

AUDRINA LANE

Copyright © 2020

DEDICATION

I would love to dedicate this book to a few people who have stuck with me since I started my writing career. Jo Morris who suggested I write about superbikes, so I hope you like it! Tania Emma Shrimpton who asked if she could be a character in one of my stories, so here you are, your wish has been granted. Miriam Baker and Nicky Lee and the rest of my lovely Audrina's Angel's Facebook group, your support is always appreciated!

Kazz Mossman for her wonderful proof reading and editing skills, and having a fellow author read and enjoy this story. Electric Eclectic Authors and group for helping to promote and support my writing. The fabulous book cover designer Eleanor Lloyd Jones of Shower of Schmidt Designs for working her magic on this amazing book cover.

TABLE OF CONTENTS

CHAPTER 1

The heat of the day had started to tail off as the cooler breeze whipped up her curls. She'd missed the sun, having been sat in a hotel conference room signing books and chatting to readers with 30 other authors. She'd had a decent day, smiled for selfies and chatted with author friends both new and old. It was always the highlight of any month to attend a book signing and feel the adoration that her words evoked. Little did they know that the men she created and the love scenes she wrote were a far cry from her real life.

Cara's sports car was her pride and joy and with the summer sun, falling like a fireball from the deepening sky, she pressed her foot to the pedal as the miles started to fly by. Next to writing and her dog, Mansell, yes named after a formula one driver, she had no one. Her hero had betrayed her for another, and she seemed destined to never meet anyone to match her exacting standards. Well, when you get to write male characters you can make them gorgeous, sexy, rich or poor, egotistical or just downright dirty depending upon your mood.

With the music on loud she followed the curve of the road, weaving in and out of the slower cars and lorries. She saw the envy from boy racers, too young to afford a Jaguar F-Type or even just the insurance and tax. They liked to over-take and she just let them until they slowed down and then she reeled them back in and left them in a plume of exhaust fumes and of course a grin and wave! It always put a smile on her face and left them looking bemused and probably frustrated.

She was slowing down for one of the major roundabouts and above the music on the stereo she heard the deep, throaty growl of something with an engine as it slowed. A motorbike pulled up beside her and a figure in-cased in black leather put his foot down and out of the corner of my eye she saw him turn his head her way. It was a fleeting second before the gap opened in the traffic and they both pulled away, he left her in his dust cloud. But then she saw him slowing down and pulling back into the traffic just in front of her. Was this biker playing games with her? Now it was her turn to overtake and, in the wing-mirror she watched as he pulled out behind to follow her past the slower moving traffic. At the set of traffic lights, they both stopped next to each other again. This time she glanced across and saw him flip up his visor to reveal a piercing set of bright blue eyes. They crinkled at the corners like he was smiling or maybe smirking inside his helmet.

It seemed like they saw her, and it made her nervous and excited in equal measure. Then the lights changed, and he flipped his visor down and pulled off slightly ahead. She was slower off the mark as her heart was pounding and her hands had started to shake on the steering wheel. Her mystery biker could again have left her in his wake, but he was only just ahead, so she floored the accelerator and caught up. Cara pulled in behind him, so she could admire his form in the tight leathers that he wore. She was now plotting her next novel in her head and her fingers itched to start writing, but she knew she would have to wait until she got home for that.

The final set of traffic lights loomed, and he was in the far lane and Cara was in the near to turn left for the last part of her journey home. He lifted his visor again, and she drank in what she thought would be her last look at this blue-eyed biker. He winked, and she licked her lips and smiled. Cara wanted those lights to stay on red forever, but they changed, and she slowly turned, not daring to look back. Why on earth was she feeling like she should just turn the car around and follow him. In the end she found the next layby and pulled over. She had a bottle of water in the boot and she needed something to calm her down. Cara leaned against the side of her car, enjoying the feel on her parched throat until it reached the heat bubbling inside. Christ, her vibrator was going to take a hammering tonight.

Then she heard the throaty, unmistakable sound of his bike again. Cara froze and started to shake, watching back down the road as her mystery man appeared over the brow of the hill and then slowed to pull in behind the car. Fuck… her breath was coming out so fast that she hic-cupped as she swallowed the last sip of water. The bottle dropped from her fingers as he climbed off the bike. Cara quickly smoothed down her sundress, it had been nice and cool, due to its floaty nature… but somehow as he removed his helmet she wished for more coverage.

Cara gulped as he tied the helmet to his bike and walked towards her. He was breath-taking. His piecing blue eyes against nicely tanned skin and bright white teeth as he grinned. His shock of black hair was ruffled from being trapped under his helmet and a soft sheen of sweat was on his forehead. He was silent as he bent down and picked up the dropped bottle, which he threw casually in the bin nearby. Then he was standing full height in front of her, she was trapped between his body and the car, looking up into his face and hoping she wasn't blushing too hard.

"Hey girl, I just couldn't let you drive by." He uttered, before moving closer as his fingers tangled in her messy curls. He pulled her closer as he slid his hand through her hair, down her neck and then a casual finger traced the line of her jaw. Cara still hadn't said a word as on tip toes she leaned in to let his lips meet hers. It was a sweet, soft brushing of closed mouths, the action taking both of them by surprise in its intensity. His eyes never left hers and she couldn't look away, instead blinking her shock at their brief encounter. Cara opened her mouth to say something, but no words came to mind, what do you say to a stranger pinning you against your car and kissing you like your souls belonged together. Instead she licked her lips and waited for him to take the not so subtle hint, which he did.

With both of his arms around her he rained tiny kisses over her cheek, neck, jaw before alighting back onto her waiting lips, she opened to him and let his tongue explore. Cara was shaking, but not from nerves just the sheer joy of their kisses. Some were short and brief, then others long and probing as they both explored. He smelt divine, a mixture of leather, sunshine and her favourite aftershave 'Cool Water'. Her hands ran down his back, over the tight leather jacket that she was sure covered a body that was taut and toned. His hand brushed down her side, catching her breast and making her nipples spring into life, like a shock of electricity to her skin. He must have felt it because he paused and looked into her eyes once more.

"What's your name?"

"Ca… Cara," she stuttered out.

"I'm Ewan and it's great to meet you." He blushed as the conversation slammed to a halt. Was this it, was this all he wanted before he drove off and out of her life. Instead he took her hand in his and they walked together to where the lay-by ended and became grass. Cara just followed his lead, she wanted more kisses, she wanted whatever he had in mind and she just hoped it was what was running through his. They followed a barely visible path in the long, dry grass and over a slight mound until the road and layby were out of sight. The sun was setting behind them, the moon rising over a small stream ahead. They found a flattened patch of grass and letting her go he unzipped his jacket, shrugging it off to lie it on the floor. He turned away and unzipped his leathers, pulling them off to reveal a nice set of legs in shorts.

Then he casually sat down and patted the space on his jacket for her. He pushed off his boots and she stepped out of her sandals and then sat down next to him. Were we going to talk or just kiss some more? She wondered.

His plain white t-shirt clung to him in all the right places and Cara couldn't resist as she turned on her side and let her fingers touch the v of the neckline before running down the material. Then catching her off balance he pulled her down atop of him, his muscles hard against her softer curves. Their lips joined again as his hands ran down her spine and then up, pulling her short hemline with them, before he started back down to grasp her ass, naked in a tiny thong. His hands were hot against her cooling skin as he rubbed in a circular motion and pushed her in tighter against his firm body. Oh my god, this guy knew what he was doing as their kisses grew deeper still and her heart started banging against her chest. Cara wanted more as she let her hands creep down his side to tug his t-shirt from the waist band of his shorts. She needed to feel his skin on hers. She pulled away from him slightly, enough to sit up as she sat astride him and dispensed with her dress.

He shadowed her move and sat up too, she was still in his lap as she helped him to pull the t-shirt over his head. Cara gasped in admiration at his firm lines and contours, just like the hero's in her books. He let out a short sigh as his hands reached around to undo the catch of her bra. The air felt cool on her skin, a breath of fresh air against the clammy evening heat. He cupped them both, letting each thumb rub

8

over her erect nipples, playing with them in a rhythm that made her sigh. Ewan was her new hero, and he was showing her what she needed to write when she got home. Removing his hands, he moved his head down so that he sucked each of them in, letting his tongue swirl around them, before leaving with a nip to move to the other. Cara ran her hands through his hair, holding him close so that he repeated the move time and time again. She arched closer to him, wanting him so much as their skin brushed against each other's, heightening the friction.

Cara was so wet, as she wiggled her frustration into his lap. He felt her burning desire as he quickly shifted so that she lay beneath him. His strong arms held her down as she lay partly on his leather's and partly in the grass. The sensations were incredible as the grass brushed her skin roughly on one side and the other felt the smoothness of the lining of his jacket. Cara saw his eyes, running down over her taut belly and then stop at her pink panties. He stared before glancing back up and Cara just nodded her approval. She needed his touch, his finger, his tongue.

Ewan's fingers pulled her string down as she shimmed so that she was naked before him. He slipped his shorts down and Cara took her first look at his cock. It was as magnificent as she imagined it to be and she wanted him even more, even though she still only knew his name. He knelt back, letting his hand run up her leg and then down the other, teasing as he inched ever closer to the prize with each sweep. Then he was there, a finger slid into her folds and she shook. Cara was so close to the edge that she knew it wouldn't take long for her first orgasm to break free. She'd been celibate, except for her vibrator and imagination for nearly two years. Once again, he looked up and smiled, enjoying the power he had over her but equally wanting this to be something they shared.

They were connected, intense slaves to their bodies wants and desires, and they just couldn't stop now. Then his tongue was there, licking and lapping as ripples became waves that engulfed Cara.

"Ewan" she cried as she shuddered onto his tongue. "Ewan… Ewan… Oh my fucking god!" Her cries echoed on the breeze as he pulled back and saw the blush on her skin. She wanted to repay the favour, but he held her down as she tried to stifle her moans. He reached across to an inside pocket on his jacket and pulled out a condom. Then he let her go and lay back down in the grass, motioning Cara to jump on top. She scrambled off the ground and took a moment to savour his masculinity. He was submitting to her desires and she adored the power exchange he gave so freely. She took a moment and leant over to suck on his sheathed cock, wanting to turn him on in the same way he'd done for her.

"I'm yours Cara" he whispered, it was the first time her name had rolled off his tongue and it sounded like music. Cara moved to straddle him, lowering down onto him with slow care. She wanted to savour this for longer as he pierced her to the core. "Fuck" they both said in unison and then laughed as she settled onto him. He was a perfect fit as she slowly started to grind against him. He lay back, arching to meet her every move and holding her tight with his hands on her waist.

"Faster," he moaned, "Ride me like you want to lose control." She nodded and increased her tempo, before feeling bold and moving his hand so that it was on her clit. His thumb pressed against the nub and then started to rub in time with the thrusts. Cara was not going to last as she flung her head back and let out a howl of satisfaction, like a wolf to the moon. The sweat was dripping off them as she rode until he went tense and came. She joined him with her third or was it her fourth orgasm, she'd completely lost count. Her whole body was on fire, bathed in the silver shimmer of the moon that was now fully in the sky. She slumped down to lie close to him, gasping for breath and lost in the moment of wild abandonment they'd just shared. Two strangers overtaken by need, fulfilling their pent-up desires on a roadside embankment.

She rolled off him as he shrunk and dealt with the condom. Then he lay back beside her and gazed at the stars above. The moment had been perfect, and she didn't need to speak as his hand slipped into hers, giving it a squeeze that she returned. A tiny acknowledgement of the intimacy that they didn't want to break with words. But then he slowly sat up to find their clothes, strewn in the grass on either side. Cara took a final long look at his body, so sculpted and raw against the surrounding countryside. Here was a man so comfortable in his own skin as he saw her look and smiled. She pulled on her knickers and sundress; the material chaffed her still tingling body.

He walked her back to their vehicles, the road next to them quiet now. She longed to give him her card, let him know she wanted a repeat but afraid that for him this was just a chance encounter. He pulled on his leathers and then paused for a moment, aware that she was watching him. He stepped back towards her, pinning her against the bonnet of the car. Cara wrapped her legs around his waist as he laid her back for a final long kiss. It was only the lights and a cheeky car horn that broke them apart.

"Take care Cara," he said, softly brushing a final kiss on my cheek "Maybe I'll drive by you again some time."

"You too Ewan." she mumbled, her heart was breaking now as he strode to his bike and pulled on his helmet. Before he pulled the visor down, she took one last look at his eyes, like a warm fresh ocean she wanted to dive into again. Then he fired up the engine and Cara watched and waved as he turned the bike around and with a flourish he was gone. Just the red of his back light blinding her as a tiny tear slid down her cheek.

Chapter 2

Cara wiped it away wanting this to remain what it was, a beautiful moment in both of their lives. Then back in her car she turned the key and drove slowly along the last few miles to pull into the drive. Her neighbour had called in to see Mansell during the day, but his eager little face greeted her as she walked through the door.

"Let's go to bed," she said, as he ran up from his business in the garden and then upstairs to take his place in his basket. Cara lay awake for a while, the memories swirling around her mind and her body still humming. The scent of him still bathed her skin and she wondered who he was? Would she ever see him again? Cara jumped out of bed the next morning, determined to get an early start on her new novel starring a hero called Ewan and his motorbike. Turning on the news she nearly choked on her coffee, as Ewan appeared, holding aloft the Superbike trophy.

At least she knew where to find him now, but did he want to be found? Was she chasing a dream that their layby moment held more promise?

Giving Mansell his breakfast and then opening the patio doors onto the garden, she let him out to sniff and play. Her dining table was her writing desk in the summer so she could look up and see her tiny garden, filled with pots of flowers and a small stretch of lawn that belonged to her tumble boy terrier. She opened her laptop and a new document, still determined to try and capture the feelings and experience of yesterday evening. But she couldn't stop from writing the title 'Drive By' and then clicking the internet icon. She hit the sports pages and found the Superbike article and of course a beaming picture of her new hero. His full name was Ewan Michaels and not only was this his first season in Superbikes, but he'd also gone and won it in a thrilling final race.

Cara clicked the video clip and watched the final 3 laps where the leader, Neil Summers had clipped one of the kerbs, flipped his bike and skidded out across the track, taking the second placed man with him. This left Ewan to overtake the startled rider in 3rd and claim first place and with only 1 point the winning margin. The whole of the racetrack had erupted in a sea of Union Jacks for their under-dog hero had triumphed. She watched him take the podium, punch the air and his grin was as wide as the one she'd witnessed the previous evening. Cara shut her eyes again, resting back in her office chair and letting the previous night's memories assault her. She even fancied that she could smell Cool Waters drift in on the slight summer breeze. Her nipples peaked and ached beneath her thin vest top and she tingled all over.

Cara put his name into the search engine next, afraid that she would find some glamourous model girlfriend in his present. But apart from a wannabe pop star from one of those reality shows, he appeared to be just like her...SINGLE. Perhaps that's how he liked it? He had

Certainly, been an expert at flirting in such a persuasive manner that she'd dropped her knickers for him faster than a lap at Brands Hatch. Cara blushed just thinking about the whole encounter, but was she filled with regrets? Only one. She should have slipped her business card into his pocket; how would he find her again? Cara gulped and stood up to grab another coffee from the machine. She was by nature a true author, slightly reclusive except on book signing occasions, and deserted layby's! She had known her last boyfriend Nigel since university. Her few friends had assumed that they would be together forever, but he had other plans. A series of flings followed for him, as she feverishly locked herself away to write her first novel. Emerging with a coveted but basic publishing deal from a small independent press and a broken heart when he left her for her then best friend Sandra.

Her first book had been successful enough for Cara to give up her full-time job and just depend upon some shifts at a local café to keep her afloat. She had found Mansell outside one evening, cowering behind the bins and after a week at the local NSPCC Centre, in case his owners came to claim him, he was adopted by her. She loved his little scruffy face and the strange black patch of fur across his nose made her think of Nigel Mansell's moustache and so his name had seemed to suit him. Cara smiled as he drew her from her thoughts with a sharp bark before he jumped in the air and tried to catch the pigeon flying over his head. She laughed and returned to the screen.

A plan was forming in her mind, but she just couldn't find the courage to take it any further.

With a blank page waited for her she started to type the words, telling of a lonely writer, with a love of fast cars and equally fast men. His blue eyes seemed to float across the page, but her fingers flew, and she just let them. Later in the day she grabbed Mansell's lead and they went out for their daily walk. Cara needed some food for supper that evening, and the local market was just the place. She was craving sweet things like her friend Tania's delicious fruit scones and a rest stop half-way round at the café where she sometimes worked was just the place. Tania saw her take the table outside at the far end of the canopies shade. It was also the spot closest to the bowl of water for thirsty dogs. Within a few minutes Tania was setting down her favourite pot of tea, two cups and three scones with jam and cream.

"Hey stranger, how was yesterday's event? You haven't put any pictures up yet?" Tania said, nodding to her other member of staff that she was taking a break.

"Oh, I guess I just forgot." Cara mumbled, feeling heat blossom on her cheeks and a slow smile spread across her lips.

"What's up with you? You're blushing and I spy a secret lurking beneath your closed lips. Spill?"

"Um… can I keep my secret a little longer. I'm just getting used to it."

"Ooooh... secret?? Is it book related? Or is it something else?"

"Let's just say I met a mysterious stranger on my way home."

"How? I thought you said you were taking the sports car this time rather than a huge pull along suitcase?"

Cara bit into the delicious, crumbly scone that she had been coating with strawberry jam and cream. Her mind already thinking of a deliciously seductive scene with Ewan and food. The heat was burning up her neck now and she knew that sooner or later she'd have to tell Tania everything, but not today.

"Mmmh, this is perfect." Cara moaned, "You are like my own personal Nigella, can I take a couple of more to go? I've just started my next novel and need to get going before the scene I'm thinking of flees my brain."

"Sure, but I think we need a girl's night in soon and I might require your waitressing service at the end of next week?"

"Sure, that's fine and shall we say next Saturday night then. You bring the food and I'll bring the wine."

"And the secret?" Tania pleaded.

"Yes."

Mansell waited as Cara dropped the final piece of scone for him to enjoy as she finished her tea. On the walk home she drifted until a motorbike swung out of a side street and she stared at it until it rounded the corner. Her heart was pumping again, and she just knew that she needed to do more research before she could commit to a plan of contact, or seduction.

CHAPTER 3

Ewan walked through the door of the flat, it felt cold and unloved. He was hardly here these days with the different races all over the world. The last few years had been a bit of a whirlwind, his big break on the bikes and now this. The weekend had been perfect, ok he would have liked to have won on his own merit but then that was racing. When the dice was thrown, and people made mistakes you had to be there to clean up and that's exactly what he had done. The team had taken his trophy with them back to the factory and after much pleading he'd been allowed to ride home on his own bike.

He turned the lamp on and then found a solitary can of lager in his rather empty fridge. He cracked it open and after discarding his leathers he flopped onto the sofa. A swift scent of something floral rose up and then he really smiled. The race and championship win had been great, but how could he forget the icing on the cake. The gorgeous blond in her red jaguar speeding along the road. She'd been too good to let go and when he'd finally found the courage to turn around and see if he could find her, she'd been there. Waiting in the layby for him.

"Cara" he breathed, letting her glorious name trip off his tongue before he took another sip of beer. It tasted sour against the cherry sweetness of her full lips, he closed his eyes and put it down on the coffee table.

She danced before his closed eyelids, her curves and the way they had felt pressed between him and her sports car. A song popped into his head, one of his favourites by the Stereophonics "The One." He shivered as the words played on his mind, after so little time could a person really fall in love. He didn't know as he'd never fallen before. "Cara." He'd satisfied his lust on that grassy embankment, beneath the moonlight but now where did he go? All he knew was her first name and that she drove an F Type Jaguar and that she was blond, with gorgeous brown eyes, like dark pools of chocolate. That she was probably not the type of girl who was that easy, but the moment earlier had just been right. He wanted to know more, he needed to know more. He just had to see her again, but how? He'd forgotten to ask her for her number, failed to tell her his full name even.

As the adrenaline started to fade, he yawned and finished his beer, then he walked to his room and stripped off. He held his t-shirt tight and took a deep inhale, her scent still lingered there. Rather than throw it on the floor he clutched it in his hand and slid beneath the cover. He tried to sleep, but all his brain would do was replay the whole of their encounter over and over again. He slipped his hand beneath the sheet and took care of the erection that had resulted from such vivid images. With the t-shirt next to him on the pillow he finally slept.

It was the phone that woke him up the next morning.

"Uuuh?" he answered, "What time do you call this?"

"Ewan, it's your Mum here. I just wanted to congratulate you on your win yesterday. Your dad would have been so proud."

He heard her voice dip at the end, and he swallowed the lump in his throat. It was only six months since his passing and it still hurt. He heard a small sob from the other end and wondered what to say next.

"I did it for him, he was my inspiration," Ewan said, feeling the burden of his father's ambitions finally lifting a little from his shoulders.

"I know you did, Ewan," she choked out.

"Do you fancy a lunch out?" he asked. "I can take you to your favourite restaurant by the river, treat you?"

"Oh, that would be perfect, are you sure you can spare the time?"

"Yes Mum, season is over and hopefully it will be quiet enough for me to not get noticed."

"Well, you're famous now. Everyone will want a piece of you so just be careful."

"Ok Mum, I'll meet you there at noon. Leave the table booking to me."

He stared at his t-shirt, now crumpled and twisted on the bed beside him. His Mum would have the answer's, she was the only woman he trusted in the whole world.

"See you later and ride carefully."

He laughed as she hung up, she'd been saying that ever since his dad had bought him his first bike when he'd turned seven years old. He picked up his phone again and scrolled to find Gray's number.

"Hey Gray, any chance of a table at your place, stick me in the corner if you can."

"Is that you, Ew? Fucking hell mate, what a ride yesterday. We were all in the bar, glued to the tv screen. Are you sure you want to still eat here?"

"Of course, I do mate, I'm no different than I was yesterday."

"Just a bit richer and more famous. Table for two or did you pull those two girls on the podium with you yesterday?"

"Nah, just me and my best girl… Mum."

"Sure, for you anything. Oh, and if you have those brunette's number's you can give them to me. I would have if it had been me!!" he snickered, and Ewan laughed. His mate had been the womaniser all the years they had been friends. Ewan was just the plain, scruffy one that girls dated to get closer to Gray.

After a quick shower he called his team boss, the

answerphone kicked in.

"Dale, Ewan here. Can you let me have a list of things I have to do before the next season. I know I'm on a break this week, but I guess I wasn't planning on winning the race or the championship. Cheers."

He hung up and then after a quick shower he pulled on some jeans and a t-shirt and opened the front door. He was almost blinded by the flash bulbs and shouting.

"A quick word about your win?"

"How does it feel to be world champion?"

He quickly shut the door again and slid down to sit on the floor of the hallway. "Fuck, what was he going to do?"

Picking up his phone he called Matt who lived in the flat below him, "Hey Matt, is there any chance I can shimmy down the fire escape onto your balcony?"

"Uh, why?" Matt asked, clearly still half pissed from the previous night.

"Because there is a fuck load of press reporters outside my door and I have to go out."

"Ok, go for it. Patio doors are still open, just be quiet cos I'm still in bed…. If you know what I mean!"

"Thanks mate, I owe you one."

"Just leave me a tip on the table," Matt laughed, and the line went dead.

Ewan grabbed his helmet and leathers from the night before and then climbed over the railings onto the fire escape down to the flat below. He crept through the lounge and left some cash on the coffee table. Then slowly he opened the door and peeped out. The stairwell was empty, but he could still hear the banging and shouting at his door above. He ran down the stairs into the basement garage, jumped on his bike and revved. It sounded perfect, his powerful purring kitten. A lone photographer appeared in the doorway of the stairwell, trying to hear his voice above the roar of the bike engine.

"He's down here," he yelled, before raising his camera. Ewan flipped down the lid on his visor and gunned it out of the parking area. First thing on Monday morning he'd be finding somewhere new to live and second, he needed a minder to protect him from this hungry horde of reporters. Out of the city he made good time on the roads, before pulling into "The Grey Man" pub and restaurant. The car park was filling up, but he slid his bike to a stop around the back. He slunk into the kitchen through the back door and saw the familiar shape of Gray.

"Thanks Bud, you're never gonna believe what happened to me this morning."

"Ewan," Gray yelled, dropping the ladle back into the saucepan and making his nearby sous chef jump out the way. The two guys embraced and Gray led him through the kitchen and into the back of the bar.

"Need a drink?"

"Just a coke thanks, I've got the bike outside and I'll have some wine with Mum."

"Sure, but I put a bottle of champagne on ice for you. You're our home-town champion now and only the best will do."

"Open it and make sure everyone here gets a glass." Ewan said, glancing around the crowded bar. "I had reporters outside my door this morning, shouting and clicking photos. I had to escape over the balcony."

"Shit mate, that's tough. But your world champion now, fucking famous like Rossi."

"I don't want the fame, just to ride and win."

"You're the most fucked up guy I know… think about it. You'll have super models falling at your feet, pop stars fawning over you. You can have any female on the planet if you want."

"I guess I'm not ready for all that yet." Ewan shrugged and

watched his mate pop the cork on the chilled bottle of Dom Perignon.

"Cheers Ewan Michaels, champion of the world." He filled the glass and gave one to Ewan, "Just one."

"Cheers." Ewan replied, resigned as Gray shouted above the music that drinks were on Ewan, champion of the village.

Chapter 4

As the champagne flowed and people came over to say congratulations, Ewan kept looking out for his mum and still the image of Cara haunted him. If she walked in here now, what would he do?

"Ewan," his mum said, tapping his shoulder so that he turned around from the small crowd gathered around.

"Mum." He reached out and they embraced. "Congratulation," she breathed, clearly bemused as the whole pub erupted into clapping and cheers.

"Let's go and sit down." He said, ushering her to the back of the restaurant and the small hidden booth. She nodded and after nodding to the bar staff to continue with the drinks, they slipped away.

"Are you alright? Did you have any reporters outside your house?" Ewan asked.

"No, but the Herald phoned me and asked for an interview."

"And?"

"I said I'd think about it."

"Well if you do, just don't get that awful photo out of me."

She laughed, the image of him as a chubby baby sat next to his dad on his Harley was the one that he hated."

"Ok love."

Over lunch he told her about the winning race and the incident with the reporters on his front door, she agreed that he needed to get a security guard and a new home if he thought it would help. He saw the way she was looking at him in the quiet moments between chat and food.

"Is there something else on your mind?"

"Maybe…" he stumbled over the jumble of thoughts in his head. "Uh… how did you know that Dad was the one?" he finally asked, her scrutinising gaze demanded the truth.

"Have you met someone?"

"Sort of Mum, it was a bit of a chance encounter, but I can't stop thinking about her."

"Well do something about it then, take her out on a proper date. Bring her round for me to meet." His Mum giggled at her last comment, but then she went silence as she saw the thoughtful look on his face.

"I wish I could, but I don't know her full name and I don't even have a phone number to contact her."

"Ewan, she's not some grubby little racetrack hussy?"

"No Mum, she's just a girl I meet on the way home."

"Well, you know how your Dad and I met, and I guess it was a chance encounter, too The feeling was just right, and everything slotted into place. If she is your one, then she'll find you. You're famous now it shouldn't be hard if she feels the same way. If she doesn't then I guess it's not meant to be." She laughed and finished her glass of red. "Hark at me, I sound like one of those romantic novels I read. Everything in a book ends happily ever after."

"Yeah Mum, and I just saw a pig fly past the window."

A couple passed their table, and the young lad held a piece of paper out and a pen. "Can I have your autograph," he asked.

"Sure, you can." Ewan replied, scribbling on the piece of paper and suddenly seeing a flash of his future and hundreds of autographs to come. Could he handle the fame, but would any girl be able too?

He walked his mum out to her car, through the crowds of well-wishers and a few more autograph hunters. Then with a wave to Gray, he climbed onto his bike. It seemed to be the only place he felt safe. He didn't want to go home yet so instead he drove back the way he had been the previous night. The layby was etched into his mind as he parked up and just sat astride his bike. Her memory was so fresh, and he just hoped his Mum was right. If she felt the same, then perhaps she'd find him.

Returning to the block of flats he took a deep breath and climbed the stairs back to the fourth floor.

He knew he could look round the corner at the top of the stairs and see if the reporters were still there. When he snuck a peep, the corridor was empty, so he sprinted to his door, turned the key and locked it behind him. As he sat down with a coffee his phone rang, it was Dale.

"How are you?" Dale asked.

"Ok, considering I had to climb out of my fire escape to get past the paparazzi outside my door this morning."

"God, I should have thought about that, but I really wasn't expecting you to win the championship in such a last-minute turn of fortunes."

"Well, neither did I." Ewan laughed as he heard his manager do the same. They had worked together for the last 3 years and Dale was always on top of things.

"Look, I know you're supposed to be taking a break for the next week, but the press has been on the phone and email to me, along with lots of other interview possibilities and product endorsements. We must start to cash in on them as soon as possible. Shall we meet in the office tomorrow morning?"

"Think we might have to. Can I head over early, say around eight and just hope I have no one camped out on my doorstep in the morning."

"I'll call for a press conference at the office for twelve so all the reporters will come there instead of hassling you at home. Talking of which I think you might need to move."

"I was thinking the same thing, anyway I'm sure you can help me spend some money on a new pad."

"Pent-house suite now mate, you'll have the ladies flocking around you like bees to the honey pot."

Ewan heard the snigger in his voice and laughed along with him, he only had one girl on his mind and he just wanted to see her again.

Finishing the call, he stared around his flat. He didn't have many possessions so moving wouldn't take long. In fact, he didn't even own the flat where he was living, just rented until he had the money to buy what he wanted. He pulled out his computer and drafted a letter to the letting agency saying he'd be leaving in the month, sooner if he could manage it. Then he logged onto his bank account and just stared at the figures in disbelief. He loved his bike, he adored racing, winning was a bonus but what did it all matter if he had no one special to share it with. With another coffee in his hand he picked up the photo album that he kept on the shelf. It was his father's memories, neatly collated by his Mum with dates and little snippets of information. His favourite photo was at the back, one of the later race meetings when he'd been old enough to start riding. They had perched him on the bike between them, the grin on his face for the photographer, but his Mum and Dad only had eyes for each other. That was the look he wanted, just all-consuming love that shone through the faded print.

Shutting it as the memory of his death came flooding back, he swallowed and bowed his head. He had to be strong, he had to be ready for the press tomorrow as the question was bound to come up. Was he ready to become the pin up boy of the bike circuit? He hardly thought it but that's what winning yesterday had done for him. When he got hungry later, he found a tin of beans and a slightly stale loaf of bread that was good enough for toast and then he had an early night.

Chapter 5

Cara tapped away on her pc for the rest of the week, this story was coming along. She'd sent a couple of sample chapters over to her editor who had just replied back with a bold 'KEEP GOING, THIS IS AMAZING!!!' When she had ventured out it was to purchase any available newspaper and magazine that featured her new hero, the one in the book and the one she couldn't forget. Ewan was everywhere after his win. Cara had adored the press conference with him on Sky Sports. He was so well spoken and even answered the difficult question about his father's recent death. It had made her remember the news story when it had come out that the retired ex-world champion had skidded off the track and died of head injuries. She had almost burst into tears watching Ewan try to control his emotions and answer that his father was the safest rider that he knew and that this freak accident was exactly that.

The shift at the café had passed in a blur, purely because when her mind was on writing she was a completely blond air head. Forgetting people's orders, dropping plates and generally making a mess of even the simplest of jobs. Luckily, Tania always forgave her and when Saturday night rolled around, Cara finished the chapter she was on and climbed into her favourite pyjama's. That was the great thing about their girl's nights, they only wore what was comfy, slouched around in their slippers and baggy cardigans, no makeup and no worries.

Tania just wandered in; her arms full of various boxes of food.

"Cara, I need a hand before I drop one of these and I know how much you love chocolate cake."

"Coming," Cara yelled, sliding along the wooden hallway and holding out her hands for one of the boxes. Then they both walked back into the kitchen where Mansell looked up from his chew and wagged his tail at his favourite visitor.

"Hey, Manse. I've got a treat for you later." Tania said, reaching to stroke his head now that all the containers and the French stick were safely on the kitchen table.

"What are we cooking tonight?" Cara asked, opening her arms for one of their girly hugs.

"Tapas to start so no cooking required, then seafood paella with toasted garlic bread and of course chocolate cake to finish. If we've got room."

"I have deliberately starved all day in preparation."

"Get the wine open and start decanting the olives, cheese and meats." Tania said, as she wandered around to the oven and started to get the pans & dishes ready for the paella.

Running some water into the pan for the rice she turned around.

"Here you go, it's a Spanish red and lovely." Cara replied, passing the glass to her friend and then popping an olive into her mouth. As they picked at the Tapas, Tania worked her magic with the seafood paella with prawns and smoked salmon. Mansell soon left his bone and wandered over to sit hopefully by the table. Cara carried the garlic bread to the table and Tania produced the main course. They were nearly onto their second bottle of red when Tania looked over at Cara.

"Please put me out of my misery, what is the secret?"

Cara swallowed her mouthful of food and blushed, almost matching the shade of the wine.

"I was very reckless on my way home from the book signing."

"Oh shit, you crashed the car?" Tania exclaimed, her hand going straight to her mouth.

"No, I'd still be crying now if I'd done that."

"You sold out of all your books?"

"Nah, but I came pretty close." Cara replied. "Look you'll never guess."

"Well tell me then, woman."

Taking a sip of wine and closing her eyes for a brief second to see an image of Ewan there, Cara looked up at her friend.

"I met someone; we had a liaison in a lay-by."

"Fucking hell shit I'd never have guessed that in a million years…. but how if you were driving the car?"

Between mouthfuls of food, Cara told Tania about Ewan. She left a few of her favourite parts out but when she finished the silence was palpable. Tania was just staring at her, mouth wide open and a look of amazement on her face.

"Well, what are you going to do about it? You know who he is, for Christ sake he's famous so you'd better get in there quick before someone else snaps him up."

"But what if he thinks I'm desperate, just another gold digger after him for his money now that he's famous." Cara looked quietly into her glass of wine. *What if she'd read too much into the final lines of wanting to drive by again? Perhaps he said that to all the girls?*

"Cara, you could never come across as a whore, no matter how hard you tried. You're too nice and that's why you're already talking yourself out of going after this guy."

"Well, what do you think I should do? Write him a letter? Turn up at the bike manufacturer's demanding to see him?"

"Ah, so you've thought of those things." Tania laughed,

taking a sip of her own wine between mouthfuls of the risotto.

"I want to be more subtle, but I really don't think I can pull it off." Cara mumbled, blushing as all her other plans scanned through her mind. The only one she felt comfortable with was trying for a chance encounter, but how did you plan those.

"I get it, you just want to kind of bump into him, look all surprised. A bit like your heroine did in the last book when she bumped into the guy in a supermarket."

"Yes, then it gives us both the chance to say goodbye in a polite way, no misunderstandings."

Getting up from the table, Tania grabbed a notepad and pen from the sideboard.

"Get your laptop out, we're playing stalkers. We need to try and find some places where he is going to be and then just make sure you're there at the same time."

Keying his name into the search bar they scrolled through from today's press conference that they had missed to nothing. Cara and Tania looked at each other, "I can't believe his team are not parading him far and wide after that win." Cara said, "Perhaps he does like his own company and no commitments."

"Perhaps it's just that this win took his management team by surprise and they are still planning publicity?"

"So, what do we do, just keep logging on every, day?"

"No, silly. We go straight for his manager. Look, there's a contact email link on his website, just press and get it open and we'll compose something now."

"Is that wise, we've had quite a bit to drink." Cara looked across at the empty bottles on the side, the 2nd had only half a glass left in it.

"No time like the present." Tania nudged her friend and grinned. "Look I'm here to help, but you're the writer."

As they opened the third bottle and enjoyed the chocolate dessert, they wrote twenty different emails, rejecting all of them as sounding desperate.

"My brain's frazzled," Tania groaned, slumping back against the sofa cushions.

"Mine too, I think I'll leave it."

"Just not too long, I don't want to be back round here with tissues when he's in Hello magazine with the love of his life who isn't you."

"Like that will happen."

"For a romance author, you're far too realistic sometimes. Dare to dream and who knows." Tania sighed, smiling at her friend, and imagining making her the best wedding cake ever.

CHAPTER 6

Walking into the office, Ewan was greeted by the entire management board, clapping his success. The trophy took pride of place in the centre of the table and another bottle of champagne was chilling in the ice bucket.

"Let's start by raising a glass to our new world champion." Dale said, popping the cork and filling their glasses.

"Thank you everyone for being such a brilliant team behind me, it's your success that we should be toasting"

They all nodded and cheered before sitting down. Some of the champagne bubbles started to go flat as the real reason for the meeting dawned on them. How were they going to capitalise on winning this championship? Ewan sat silently as the ideas started to filter out. Their PR girl, Deborah jotted everything down before chiming in. "I've booked the press for noon today, but I have emails from various motorbike, motorsport and just general sports magazines asking for interviews."

"Deborah, my diary is officially yours just book me in."

"That's great news Ewan, you're in demand."

With a clear plan of action for the next couple of weeks the clock ticked slowly towards 12noon, it was making Ewan very nervous. He felt the sweat forming on his forehead and stood up, motioning that he was heading to the men's room. Inside he tried to calm his breathing, this was all too much to take in, but he had too. Afterall this could be it, his only championship. He washed his face and then dried it, before looking in the mirror. Reflected there was an image of Cara, her hair messy and laid out on the grass. After all this mayhem and publicity, he knew he needed to find her.

Walking back into the room he saw Dale stand up and straighten his own suit and tie.

"Are you ready?"

"As I'll ever be." Ewan gulped and they walked out into the conference room and the waiting press. The hour passed in a blur as he was asked every question they had discussed previously along with some very random ones, like 'What was his favourite breakfast?' 'Did he sleep in the buff?' and even a request for him to do a photo shoot for GQ Magazine. He had shrugged and agreed, worried about what he'd let himself in for. He'd seen the Lewis Hamilton cover not long ago of his naked torso and tattoo's. There was no way he was going to get that ripped in the next couple of weeks, depending on when they scheduled it for.

With his diary full of interviews, Ewan was glad to escape and he went straight to the local estate agent. He needed a new place to live and wanted something between the capital and his mum's place so he could really escape the hustle and bustle of city living. He was a country boy at heart. The Estate agents were quiet, so he wandered around and looked at a few of the details on the walls, mansions and penthouses were just not his style. The young girl at the desk finished her phone call and walked over to him.

"Can I help you?"

"I hope so, I need to buy a house, well more of a cottage to be exact."

"Sure, have you already seen something that you like? or would you like to have a look at what's on our books?"

"Please," Ewan replied, following her back to the desk where he could sit down. Either she was a good actress, or she didn't read the papers or watch television. It was a relief as she started to take down his details. Then a guy in a suit appeared behind her, did a double take and said.

"Oh my god, are you THE Ewan Michaels?"

"Uh, yes." He said, feeling the heat of embarrassment on his cheeks.

"Katie, I'll handle this from here." He replied, extending his hand "I'm Alex, the manager."

As Katie vacated her seat, a shocked look on her face. He turned to her. "Can you get us both a drink, tea or coffee Mr Michaels?"

"Black coffee, thanks."

"Make that two and can you put my phone on divert to the spare desk."

Katie nodded, smiled and efficiently went about her tasks.

"That race was blinding, I've been a super bike fan for years so this is like a dream come true for me to actually meet you like this."

Ewan fished in his jacket pocket and found one of his new photo cards that the office had given him. He grabbed the pen and scribbled his signature onto it, sliding it across the desk. Alex grinned like a boy with a new toy but then went back into business mood.

"So, what are you looking for, price range, just let me know and I'm sure I can find you a new home."

"Well, it has to be detached, somewhere between here and Oxford with some land and a garage."

"What's the budget?"

"Top end around £800,000 but I could stretch for the right place." Ewan replied, amazed that he could happily say that figure.

Turning the computer screen to face his client, Alex scrolled through the properties that were available and then emailed them over to Ewan's address.

"Can I take a look and get back to you, I'd like to make sure I have someone with me when I look around them."

"Ah, so there is a woman in your life?" Alex enquired.

"Yes, but not the romantic variety. I trust my Mum's opinion."

Standing up Ewan shook hands and left. He pulled his phone from his pocket and rang his Mum.

"Can I come over, I'm looking at houses and I'd like your thoughts before I go and look at any."

"Yes love, I'm making cottage pie for tea and you know me, I'm no good at just cooking for one."

Ewan smiled and climbed onto his bike, enjoying the anonymity of the ride to his childhood home.

After food they checked out all the properties and reduced

the list from ten to four. Ewan phoned Alex and arranged to view them all at the end of the week, as he had a few interviews before then.

"Why don't you stay here?" his Mum asked, as she poured the wine with their food.

"Go on then," he relented, "But I'll be up early as I have some magazine interviews to attend and an interview on Radio 5."

"You just get up and go when you need too."

As Ewan finished his food he let his mind float back to Cara, something was telling him that his mum would just love her and he just had to hope and pray that she would get in touch with him.

Upstairs in his old room, he grinned at all his trophies still on the shelf, a pile of bike magazines next to them and even a faded photo on the wall of his father. Lying in bed he went back to that day. Everything had happened in slow motion, like a film clip done for dramatic effect. His Dad had been riding in a classic race at Donnington but had been recovering from an operation and had taken some tablets just before the start of the race. Now his father had usually been a stickler for checking his bike in the final ten minutes before the start but this time he'd been collared by a reporter who wanted a few words about his son following in his footsteps on the race track. Relenting he had spoken to the reporter and then climbed on his bike with minutes to spare before the flag went down. It had been a fluke accident, from what Ewan remembered, but his father's helmet had flown off at the moment of impact as his bike had slid into his nearest competitor on a bend.

The impact with the ground and then his bike had knocked him out and he never regained consciousness.

Ewan sobbed into his pillow as he remembered his mother screaming and falling to the ground, right next to him. He'd picked her up and held her, but she had just crumpled against him, "No" her only words. After a week in a coma the Doctors had advised that there was no sign of him coming back to them and they had made the decision. Ewan had not even been sure at the time if he'd ever get back on a bike but it had made his dad so proud to say that he was a racer, cut from the same cloth, that he knew he couldn't let him down. Every race he felt his father's presence beside him, urging him on and that's what he had done.

In her own room, his Mum picked up her latest book. It was a new writer to her but was certainly a fun read. She had picked it up from the local store and had been delighted to discover that the author was talking at the literary festival in a month's time. She had booked her tickets and she was looking forward to dragging her friend Beth along.

CHAPTER 7

Cara had spent the whole week tapping like a woman possessed. A photo of Ewan was on the office wall, his blue eyes making her fingers fly. She still hadn't written the email to his manager yet, afraid that everything she wrote sounded either lame or desperate. His interview on Radio 5 had been great, she had closed her eyes and just listened to the sound of his voice. She wasn't really taking in anything that he was saying, because her heart was thumping, and her mind was just back at the lay-by. She'd actually been back there once, parking her car and walking back to the spot. Then she had discovered that he was doing a photo shoot for GQ magazine and she just happened to know the photographer Cindy. Picking up her phone she pressed the number and waited.

"Hey Cind, how are you?"

"Cara, it's been a while. Do you need to book a shoot for your next book cover?"

"Uh, not quite yet but it won't be long as the words are flying."

"Great, if you send me the synopsis soon, I'm sure I can find the right models for you."

"Thanks, but that's kind of not why I'm calling."

"Ooh, tell me then?" Cindy said.

"Are you doing the photos of the superbike guy next week?"

"I think so…why do you want to know?"

Cara took a moment, surely Cindy would guess from the tone of her voice. She couldn't just come out and say that she needed to get this guy's number.

"Uh… my friend wants his autograph."

"Well, I'll try for you, most of these famous guys don't want to give you the time of day."

"No problem, I'll see you soon."

"Yeah, Cara. Don't leave it so long."

Hanging up Cara looked up to the ceiling 'Shit' she'd bottled it and hadn't even asked what time he was going to be there. She could have planned to just arrive as he was leaving. She was an idiot who didn't deserve him anyway.

Grabbing Mansell's lead, she whistled, and he came running.

"Let's go and see Tania, I'm in need of a hot chocolate and a cream cake."

Mansell wagged his tail as she pulled on her coat and left the house. She needed a break as the scene she was on was so hot it was making her squirm with pent up desire.

Tania saw her take a seat and rushed over "Hey, have you sent that email yet?"

"No, so just get me a hot chocolate and a slice of whatever is the most calorific."

"Of course, I'll be right back. Emma can handle the customers while I take a break."

Sitting down next to Cara, Tania noticed the worry lines of her mate's brow. This guy was really eating away at her friend and Tania knew she had to do something to help.

"Look, shall I come over this evening and take another look at that email over a glass of wine?"

"I just don't think I should chase him; I'm going to sound like some desperate woman, what if I was just a little roadside fling."

"Come on, since he won has, he been in the press with other women?"

"Nope, but he'd doing a GQ photo shoot next week. I was trying to find out the time, but I forgot to ask my friend Cindy when it was."

"You goof, ring her back?"

"No."

"Text her then?"

"She probably won't be allowed to tell me anyway; these famous shoots are always kept quiet to avoid eager fans."

"You mean you?" Tania laughed, giving her friend a nudge as she dropped a piece of cake on the floor for Mansell to scoop up. Seeing her friend's phone on the table, Tania grabbed it and found the last number dialled. She quickly opened up the messages and tapped away before pressing send.

"Well I've just asked."

A few minutes later Cindy replied "Since it's you Cara, he'll be here next Wednesday. I don't know the times yet though."

Tania typed "Thanks x" and handed the phone back to her friend, a bemused look on her face.

"So next Wednesday you're going to put on your best clothes and hang around outside the studio and if I wasn't so busy here, I'd come with you. But it might not work if I'm there."

"Thanks Tania, I don't know what I'd do without you." Cara replied, hugging her friend.

"So how is the new book coming along?"

"It's literally racing along; I don't think I've ever been so driven." Cara started to laugh as suddenly the name of the book flashed into her mind.

"You've got a strange look on your face, what now?"

"It's called Drive By."

"Ooh, fab title."

"Talking of which, I really need to get back to it. Come round after work as I'll order a takeaway and we can discuss what I should wear for a chance meeting."

Back at home, Cara opened the door for Mansell and watched as he sniffed around in his favourite places. Then she opened her laptop and went back to her writing, suddenly the sex scene seemed even more real.

Closing her eyes for a brief second, she imagined him pulling her close and his lips on hers once more. If only!!!

CHAPTER 8

The house viewings had gone really well and with the help of his mum he'd made the decision. He just had to go into the office and finalise the paperwork after his photoshoot on Wednesday and then wait for a moving in date. He'd paid a bit more for a quick turnaround which the vendors had been pleased with as it meant they could move into their new build before they went on holiday.

Most of the interviews had gone smoothly and Dale had told many of them that the subject of his father was off limits and they had kept to it. He'd been to the gym a few times to try and get his muscle definition a bit sharper ready for the photo shoot. His mum had been excited about his house buying and had also told him she was off to a book signing for this new author she'd been reading called C M Bennet.

On Wednesday morning he'd taken the short ride to the gym, worked out and then tried to eat breakfast but his stomach was churning with nerves. Semi naked photoshoots were most certainly out of his comfort zone.

Turning up at the studio he parked his bike and walked in, trying for the air of calm nonchalance but failing when he saw all the people getting the setting ready. A blond walked over to him and held out her hand "I'm Cindy, the photographer for the shoot. Here to make you look gorgeous for all our readers."

Next to come over was the make-up team and then the wardrobe people who took him away to get ready but not before he'd noticed the Harley sitting centre stage.

Why did it have to be a Harley they had chosen? Was it just coincidence or did they know about his father? In wardrobe Charles arranged the look they were wanting.

"We kind of want rugged boy next door, if you know what I mean?"

"Not really," Ewan shrugged as he looked at the plain white t-shirt and jeans being held out for him.

"We'll take a few of you in this and then obviously take the t-shirt off and maybe unbuckle the top button on the jeans, you know giving a glimpse but not too much."

Ewan nodded and took off his own black t-shirt and jeans to pull on the blue ones and the white t-shirt. They fitted perfectly and after the make-up artist had done a final ruffle of his hair and sprayed it, he was ready. Cindy tried to put him at ease straight away with a couple of him looking at the Harley before she wanted him sat astride.

"You are killing this," she breathed as they took a breather and she motioned for him to remove his t-shirt. If she hadn't been married, then this boy was hot! However, Cindy had a rule that she never mixed business with pleasure and as her husband was also a photographer, she stuck to the rules because he did.

"I have a friend who'd love your autograph" she said.

"Sure, remind me at the end as I have a brain like a sieve sometimes." Ewan replied, feeling quite at ease with this photographer.

"Now, I want you lounging on the bike. Stretched out as far as you're happy with."

Ewan did as he was asked but felt stiff and out of place as this was definitely not how he'd ever sat on a bike before. Cindy sensed it as she smiled and said, "If it helps think of a woman you fancy, you know those sexy thoughts about getting her to just jump on you." She giggled as she said it, remembering how many times she had used them for other people, generally the book covers she did for Cara.

As she said the words, Ewan immediately thought of Cara, she popped into his head as he remembered her astride him, her hair blowing in the breeze as her skin turned pink.

"That's perfect." Cindy said as she snapped away. "Uh, can you just reach your hand down so that it's by your waist band."

Ewan nodded, now far away in his own private daydream and the only thing holding him back was the fear of an erection on a photo shoot. In the end he just closed his eyes and enjoyed the few minutes of his daydream.

"Perfect, you're a natural." Cindy said, waking him from his thoughts. "If you ever stop riding bikes, I can get you some work on covers for an author I know. She loves her men tall, dark and sexy. Ewan laughed nervously "I don't think so and I kind of hope I have a few years of riding left."

"Well, if you change your mind here's my number." She handed him the card and in return he signed one of his photos for her before he left. "For your friend."

"Thanks, a proof copy will be with your management team by the end of today, we have to move fast so if you can agree the ones you're happy with that will make our life easy".

He nodded and left the building, seeing his trusty bike waiting for him and thankfully no press. It was like a weird game of cat and mouse with them. He climbed onboard and pulled on his helmet, he was already thinking about his next interview for 'Ride' magazine. He paused at the corner and checked his mirrors and thought he saw a red sports car pulling in. He rode away, part of him thinking back to his chance encounter in the layby. Would he ever meet Cara again?

***

Cara had spent the morning in a conflicted state, after a rather long breakfast where she debated if she would go, she then showered and spent nearly an hour trying on clothes and discarding them. Cindy had dropped her a text saying the shoot was between 11am and mid-day. What did you wear for a chance encounter? In the end she pulled on her leather look leggings and a loose but off the shoulder top with her black pumps. Grabbing her bag Mansell looked up from his basket, a mournful expression on his face. "I promise I'll take you to the café this afternoon," she said, finding him a few biscuits and tossing them into his bowl.

The traffic was calm for the first few miles into London and she enjoyed the drive. It was a lovely day and she put the top down on the car to keep cool. She was sweating already about what she was going to do, say or if she would just drive by and bottle it at the last minute. As she got closer the traffic started to build up, the clock on the dashboard was closer to 12noon now.

Then the sound of sirens from behind made her check the mirrors, it was a police car followed by an ambulance, *Shit. There must be an accident ahead.*

She pulled her car into the other lane and with the other road user's let them through. She had no choice this was the only road that led to the studio, she'd passed the turn off for the other road a mile back. As the traffic stopped in both directions Cara had a clear space to make a U-Turn and head back for the alternative route as other cars and vans did the same.

Now she really was sweating as she realised the next possible opportunity, she had just to see Ewan in the flesh, might be slipping away. As she turned the corner into the parking lot, she just caught a glimpse of a motorbike pulling off onto the road she would have been on. She didn't stand a chance of catching him up in the traffic, even if the roads were still clogged up from the accident, a bike could weave in and out. Sitting in the car park she leant against the steering wheel, trying not to cry at how close she had been. Maybe it was not meant to be? Before she had time to re-start her engine a familiar figure appeared in the doorway, did a double take and then came over.

"Hey, Cara your friend must be really desperate for that guy's autograph. Mind you if I wasn't married, I'd be there." Cindy giggled. "Do you want to come in for a coffee and I might just let you see the photos".

"Sure, I was just passing on my way to see my editor. My next book is practically writing itself and I'm hoping I can get a fast turnaround and get it out to my readers at my next book signing event in a couple of months."

Cara hoped that Cindy had not guessed that the signature was for her as she sat on the sofa and waited for Cindy to bring over the tea. Cara saw the Harley Davidson parked in the corner of the studio and went over for a closer look; she swept her hand over the leather seat imagining Ewan sad astride. Fuck, even that thought was making her heart flutter and a tingle start deep within her core.

"Cool bike," Cindy said, interrupting her daydream. "Come over here and take a look at some of the photos. I offered him the chance to do some more modelling, but he said he hoped he had a bit longer racing."

"Was he good?" Cara murmured, pulling away from the bike and back towards Cindy.

"A bit stiff to start with but he soon loosened up. I told him to think about a woman he fancied, and I captured that yearning completely. Lucky girl!"

Cara stopped mid sip and then tried to stop coughing as the liquid heat burned her throat. She was already too late, he had someone else and she was just a passing fancy. A quick hit to fill the adrenaline high of his win. Cindy hadn't noticed as she was tapping away on her laptop before moving it so that Cara could see the screen. The phone rang just as Cindy started to scroll through the images. "Take over Cara, guess I'd better see who needs me." With a shaking finger, Cara started to look at the photographs. Each one revealing more of the body that she had been lucky enough to caress.

"Ooh, you look a bit hot and bothered!" Cindy remarked, as she sauntered back over and peeped at the screen. "He's certainly got the look," Cara murmured.

"Hey, because you're a good client I'll sent you that one via email, but it's for your eyes only. If he or GQ magazine find out, I'll be shot." Cara nodded and finished her coffee, slipping the signed photo into her bag before any more interrogations. "Well, I guess I'd better get on my way now, thanks for the autograph you're a star."

"Anything for my best client, do you want to look at dates yet for your next cover?" Cindy asked.

"I'll wait and see what my editor says and get back to you." Cara replied, feeling more in need of a cold shower and a private date with her laptop than the actual meeting with her editor. Luckily it wasn't until the afternoon, so she had time for a quick sandwich and chat with Tania. "Hopefully, I'll see you soon as I need a new book to read!"

Cara giggled as she left the studio, it was amazing what a free signed book and goodwill could get you. Back in the car she dropped Tania a quick message. **Calling in for lunch, is your parking space free?** Tania was quick to reply. **Sure, just come through the kitchen and I'll have your usual ready.**

The roads had cleared so Cara was soon outside the café and ducked in through the open door.

"How did it go?"

"Don't ask, my timing sucks!"

Tania followed Cara through and poured them both some Elderflower juice and picked up the sandwich she had made. Tania let her friend take a few bites before she waded in. "So, did you see him, did he say anything? What happened?"

"I got stuck in traffic, missed him by seconds as I just caught a glimpse of a bike leaving the car park."

"You didn't chase him?"

"If you had seen the traffic around there you'd understand. Easier for a bike to weave in and out so I didn't bother to try."

"You let him get away?"

"Yeah, but from what Cindy said when I called in the studio, he already has a woman in his life. He must be keeping her secret or something." Cara turned away from her friend's prying eyes. Tania didn't need to see the hurt and pain there. Tania let her friend take a moment as she went back to the counter to take another order and returned just as the phone on the table pinged. Cara picked it up and blushed as the image appeared in the email from Cindy.

"Are you sure you're telling me everything?" Tania said, trying to sneak a peep over her friend's shoulder. "Yes, I'm telling you everything. I might as well give up now and just content myself with my writing hero's."

"Look, until you see a picture of him with someone else, I think you need to keep trying. Don't be a quitter or you might regret it." Tania laughed, realising that the line had come straight out of Cara's last book. Cara looked up and saw her friend struggling to control her giggles. "I guess I should be more like Amanda, she was a feisty one."

Cara finished her lunch and then stood up to go. "Why don't you come to this talk I'm doing at the weekend and we'll go out for dinner afterwards. There's a pub nearby and I've checked out the reviews and it's supposed to be the best?"

"Ok, sounds like a chance to have a better catch up and plot your next move." Tania replied, giving her friend a hug.

Cara's meeting with her editor went well and after picking up some extra copies of her latest book ready for the talk she was on her way home. Mansell was waiting at the door, so she grabbed his lead and took him straight out for a walk.

CHAPTER 9

Ewan picked up the keys for his new cottage and with the help of Gray and his car he was soon packed and ready to move it. Most of the furniture was new and as it arrived on the lorry, he directed them to drop it in the various rooms. Gray looked around and sighed. "All you need now is a good woman and you're set for life!"

"I have a good woman; she just happens to be my Mum!" Ewan joked, as an image of Cara popped up in his mind. "That's not what I meant, with this place and your win the world of women is your oyster, and I don't mind helping you pluck a pearl or two!" "Yeah, but you find that sort of thing easy." Ewan said, thinking of all their teenage years. "Nah, you're the celebrity now, I just own the pub and restaurant down the road." They both laughed as Gray cracked open a couple of bottles of beer and handed one over. "Now, let's get this house sorted and you can spend the evening in the bar."

"I'll come over later, I have to drop my Mum off at some book thing she's going to this evening. Then I'll need a place to hang out before I fetch her when it finishes. She hates driving at night."

"Such a good boy!" Gray laughed as they clinked bottles together and enjoyed the cold beer as more furniture arrived in the house. Gray left to open his bar and restaurant and Ewan completed the finishing touches on his new home before he jumped on his bike. The drive to his Mum's was smooth and quiet for a Saturday night and he exchanged his bike for the keys to her little Micra. Fair play, no one was going to spot him in this thing!

"Now, it finishes at around 9pm so try not to be late if you're going to be hanging out with Gray." His Mum said as she got out of the car by the Library door.

"I'll be early Mum." Ewan said, watching the different people arriving for the talk. "Oh look, Beth is waiting for me." His Mum said, clutching her bag "I'm so excited to be here, this author is one of my favourites."

"What's her name?" Ewan asked, casually. "C L Bennett, and I can't wait to meet her." His Mum gushed before she walked across to the doorway. Ewan drove straight to the bar and slipped in the side door, finding his usual table at the back, empty and waiting for him. Gray saw him arrive and came over. "Do you want the menu or the house special?"

"The steak will do and a glass of red or a bottle if you're joining me?"

"We're having a quiet night so I'll join you and we can plan your big housewarming party."

"What party?"

"The one I think you need to have so I can get you laid at least before the next race season starts." Gray chuckled, clicking his finger as his waitress passed by. He only needed to nod, and she knew what he wanted.

****

Cara pulled up outside the library and took a deep breath, book signings were one thing but actually talking about her book and answering questions was quite another. Tania looked over "Are you feeling alright? You look a bit pale?"

"Yeah, just nervous, I'll be fine once I'm inside."

"Worried all these ladies are going to be pestering you for advice on love?" Tania laughed, as Cara parked the car and they both started to get the boxes unloaded. Once inside they were shown to a table and while Tania unfurled the book banner, Cara started to put her books out on display. She couldn't wait to finish her current book so that she had more than just two books available to purchase. The chairs facing her were about half full but looking towards the door Cara saw more women arriving and it was a good mix of ages. She smiled at the two ladies taking seats on the front row, they looked about her Mum's age. The one was already clutching a copy of her first book so hopefully there would be a sale for her second when she was finished talking. The head librarian, Miss Tessler, walked over and shook hands. "It's so great to have you with us this evening. We have had lots of enquiries so are hoping for a full house."

"It's a pleasure to be here."

"Is there anything I can get you before you start?"

Cara gulped, she felt that nervous sickness feeling in the pit of her stomach "Just some water and an extra chair for my friend who will be helping with any sales later."

"Absolutely, Miss Bennett."

"Just call me Cara." She murmured in reply, before turning back to help unpack her promotional keyrings, bookmarks and pens. Once the table was set, Cara pulled out her notes, and had a last minute read through while they waited for the last few people to arrive. After Miss Tessler introduced her, Cara stood up and took a deep breath before she started to talk about writing, her first book and also her follow up. After thirty minutes she was ready for a break as she opened up to questions from the audience. It was the usual mixture of where did you get your inspiration from? Who is your favourite character, author, food and she even got to talk about Mansell her pet dog. The final question came from one of the two ladies sitting in the front row. "So, what is your next book going to be about?" she asked. Cara grinned, she loved being able to give them a little teaser, so she replied. "Well, it's a departure from my usual village romances as it focuses on an author who has a chance encounter on her way home from a book signing. She then has to discover who the man is and where she can find him again."

"Ooh, that sounds like an interesting storyline. I'm looking forward to it already." The lady in the audience replied. "Well, I hope that it will be hitting the shops before Christmas if not a little sooner." Cara replied, blushing as she thought about how the idea came about. Luckily, there was no time for any further questions on that front as Mrs Tessler clapped her hands and the audience followed suit.

"There are refreshments available to the side and you can now come over and purchase or have any books signed with Miss Bennett…oh I mean Cara."

Moving to the seat just to the side of the table, Tania stood behind it as a few eager readers came over and started to pick up the free items and buy the books. With Tania taking the payments it meant that Cara could chat and sign for each customer's and pose for a few photos. The lady who had asked the last question was talking to her friend over a drink and piece of cake, her own book still clamped firmly under her arm. But as the crowds grew less, she walked forward and picked up the second book and paid Tania for it.

"Hey, it's lovely to meet you at last and get your second book." The lady gushed, holding out both for Cara to sign. The copy of the first book looked well-worn so Cara reached across and picked up a new copy of it. "It looks like you've read it a few times so here's a replacement. Who can I make them out too?"

"My name's Jean and thank you so much, I'm a big fan and can't quite believe you're a local girl and so lovely as well." She replied, as she watched Cara scribble a message and sign both the books. "Thanks Jean, I hope you enjoy the next book." Cara smiled. As she was about to walk away her friend stopped her. "Why don't you have a picture with the author, I think I can manage to take one on the phone."

Tania watched as she peered closely at the mobile phone screen and as there were no more people waiting, she stepped forward. "Shall I do the honours then you can both be in it?" she suggested.

"Oh yes please, can you take one on my phone too. I'm hopeless with it but my son likes me to have one. He'll be amazed when I show him, I have a photo on it." Jean said, handing hers to Tania as well. With both ladies either side of Cara, Tania snapped away and then showed them both the result and how to find them later in the menu system.

"Thank you again, I hope you'll come and do another talk when your next book comes out."

"I think I might have too," Cara replied, smiling happily at the two ladies as they walked out. It took less time to pack up as they had sold most of the copies of the first book and over half of the second. She left a copy of each with Miss Tessler for the library shelves and then they were finally out.

"God, I'm in need of good food and wine now," Tania said, slipping into the passenger seat of the Jaguar. "Yes, me too. I've been told this place nearby has great reviews as the owner is the chef too."

"Get me there then, this girl needs sustenance." Tania laughed, as the engine roared and they sped off down the road.

Once in the pub car park Cara relaxed, "Those two ladies at the end were lovely, although she might find my next book a bit racier than the other two." Cara giggled. "Ah, I'm sure she's a woman who is open minded, I wonder what her son's like?"

"Not now Tania, I just need a nice meal and a glass of wine before I can go home and get back to my writing," Cara sighed, as they walked in and were shown to a table in the corner. Tania was enjoying the atmosphere as she realised the place had an open kitchen. Then she spotted the chef and her jaw dropped. "Oh my god, if that's the chef," she gasped, grabbing Cara's arm, and seeing her look in the same direction. "It has to be, he seems to be the one shouting at everyone." Cara replied, as the waiter bought over the bottle of wine and they placed their orders.

Cara picked the seafood chowder with a side of cheesy, garlic bread. Tania picked the steak, medium rare and some chips. The waiter opened the wine and poured for them, as Cara took a sip she sank back into the cushioned seat.

Their arrival had not gone un-noticed by Grayson in the kitchen, after trying to spend some time with Ewan, in between cooking, he had finally gotten a secret out of him. He'd met a girl on the way back from the race but all he knew was that she drove a Jaguar Sports car. Was there a chance that one of the two women who he had seen getting out of a red Jaguar and walked in was the same girl or was that just too much of a coincidence. Gray was rather taken with the brunette who he noticed had been checking him out from their table. As the steak and chowder were nearly finished, he quickly washed his hands and nodded to the kitchen staff to start finishing up as service was over. Casually he wandered to the bar and ordered his favourite short. He chatted to Sonia his bar maid and watched as the waiter served the two women. Giving them some time to savour a few mouthfuls he then walked over and watched the pink blush spread over the brunette's cheeks.

"Is everything to your satisfaction?" he asked, giving them both the benefit of his perfect smile.

"Yes thanks, the chowder is amazing." Cara said, tearing another piece off her bread to dunk in the creamy liquid.

"And your steak?" he turned to Tania, who was just trying to swallow the last piece. "Oh yes, it's delicious. I saw you cooking it, and I'm Tania by the way." She stuck out her hand and instead of Gray just shaking it he bought it up to his lips for a continental style kiss on the back of her hand.

"It's delightful to meet you Tania, I'm Grayson but everyone just calls me Gray." He swivelled slightly to take in Cara who was still eating. Tania noticed she had her mouthful and replied, "My friend is the well-known novelist C L Bennett, or Cara for short."

"Well, ladies I will leave you to finish eating but if you need anything just give me a shout. I'm the owner so I like things to be perfect for all my guests." He said, before nodding and returning to take a stool at the bar.

"Oh my god, he is utterly gorgeous." Tania whispered over to Cara. "Ummh, yeah he's alright I suppose. Not really my type as he seems to be a bit too smooth."

"Well what do you know miss I haven't had a date in years!" Tania replied, "I'm going to call him over again when I've finished the food. It really is delicious and I'm desperate to try this Guinness cheesecake for dessert so I can fathom out the ingredients."

Silence reigned as the girls finished their food and the waiter took their order for dessert, Cara chose the souffle and Tania the cheesecake. After a couple of mouthfuls Tania put her fork down and motioned in the direction of Gray, who saw her and wandered over.

"Is anything the matter?" he saw her part eaten cheesecake. "Yes, it's not really moist enough although the taste of the Guinness gives it a lovely flavour. I would have added more cream and maybe a dash of chocolate syrup or used chocolate cookies for the base." Tania said, watching his expression. Men normally hated being told how to do things, especially cooking.

"Sorry about my friend," Cara butted in "She runs a café in

town and she really does know what she's talking about when it comes to cakes of all kinds."

"Yes, they are my speciality" Tania boasted, watching the bemused look on Gray's face.

"Is that so? Thanks for your suggestion as I need to make another for tomorrow afternoon. We have a band playing and my Sous chef is in charge. Perhaps you'd like to be my guests?"

"Yes please," Tania replied immediately. She smiled and looked over at Cara who was just licking the spoon from her dessert.

"I'm not sure, wouldn't I be a bit of a third wheel?" she asked.

"Not if I invite my friend along. He's a bit shy sometimes but it will do him good to have a break from his mad life right now."

"Ooh, double date then!" Tania said and then blushed thinking that no mention of a date had actually be made by Grayson.

"Well, I'd certainly like to pick your brains about some of my other desserts and I love a strong opinionated woman." He leant down and ran his hand across the back of Tania's chair, casually brushing the skin of her neck. Cara watched her friend blush again, whilst mouthing 'please say yes' at her.

"Sounds perfect" Cara replied, glad to see her looking happy. As an author you never knew what could present itself in any situation and as Drive By was nearly finished, she needed an idea for her next novel.

"Can I arrange a cab to bring you over?" Gray asked, taking the seat next to Tania.

"Of course," she replied, as Gray pulled out the order pad and pen he kept in his waistcoat pocket to write down the details. "Shall I come to your place as it's easier to park?" Tania asked Cara.

"Yes, that's fine." Cara replied, rummaging in her bag for her purse to pay the bill. She was just reaching to pick it up when Gray beat her too it.

"Call it my treat," he said. Cara arched her eyebrows but neither of them saw it as they were both deep in some private conversation. Clearing her throat, she stood up and Tania noticed. "I'm afraid it's been a long day and I need to get home."

"Sure," Gray replied, letting go of Tania's hand and allowing her to stand up.

"It's been so nice meeting you and the food was delicious," Tania said, as he lent in to kiss her cheek.

"The pleasure was all mine ladies; I'll send the cab to fetch you around two tomorrow afternoon."

CHAPTER 10

"What have you got me into?" Cara said, as she started the engine and they sped out of the car park.

"I don't know, but he covered our meal and we're both on a date tomorrow afternoon. Can't you be excited for once?"

"Not really, who knows what his mate is going to be like?" Cara replied, as she negotiated the narrow lanes towards the main road and home. All she really wanted to do was to sit down and finish her novel rather than have to chat to a guy she'd never met while Tania fell into the arms of Gray.

"He was so gorgeous, well-spoken and actually listened to my suggestions about his dessert." Tania gushed.

"He was charming and rather full of himself." Cara retorted, but she still smiled at her friend and hoped that her assumptions were wrong. Dropping Tania off she smiled and blew her friend a kiss. "What time are you coming over tomorrow?" she asked.

"I'll be early, say around eleven so that I have time to get prepared." Tania said, smiling broadly.

"Fine, I'll make sure the coffee is on, if you're really lucky I might have finished the first draft of the next book."

"I'll bring that handbag of mine that goes with your poppy print dress, I think you should wear that tomorrow."

"If you wish, I'll decide on the day." Cara said, giggling that her friend had the audacity to pick her outfit for the date. On the way home all Cara could think about was the ending to her book, she still wasn't sure if what she had in mind was too cheesy and un-realistic. Mansell was waiting at the door for her and after a quick walk down the lane he was happy to curl up in his basket under the table while she tapped away at the keyboard. It was gone 2am when she finally typed "The End" and let Mansell out for a last wee before bed. She was so tired that as soon as her head hit the pillow, she was asleep, no time to even worry about the blind date for tomorrow afternoon.

***

Gray grabbed his phone as he watched the girls leave the car park, the brunette was not driving so in a way that was good because if the other girl turned out to be Ewan's mystery woman then he was going to score double tomorrow. He typed out a message **Ewan, you have a date tomorrow. Be over at the pub for 12noon and I will fill you in.**

***

Ewan felt his phone buzz in his pocket as he was pulling up outside his new house. He could still hardly believe he owned this, but it made him happy. His Mum had been full of the book talk, so he'd gone in for a coffee with her. The author she had been to see was called C L Bennett and he'd nearly spilt his coffee when she said she was called Cara. His Mum had then tried to show him a photo on her phone, but the screen had gone blank as it said no power and switched off. "Show me another day" Ewan said, trying to stay calm but his mind was racing. What if this Cara was his Cara? Was it going to be that simple?

"Look, she gave me another copy of her first book because mine was looking a bit battered." His Mum said, holding up

the paperback called "Love beneath the crooked lamppost."
Ewan took it and glanced at the sentimental cover, then at
the back but there was no author picture.

"You can borrow it if you like?" his Mum said.

"I'm not sure it's quite my cup of tea."

"Take it, I have another copy now." Jean smiled, almost
certain that this woman could possibly be the one that her
son had met on the roadside.

"Ok, look I have to get going now. I have a session with
my trainer tomorrow morning at 10am so I'd best get some
sleep."

"Of course," his Mum said, leaning in and giving him a hug
and kiss. "Take care on the way to your new home."

"I will," he murmured.

Opening his front door, he walked into the large entrance
hall, his footsteps echoed on the wooden flooring. So, this
was how it felt to own a house. Pulling open the fridge he
grabbed a beer and then flopped onto his new sofa that was
pretty comfortable. He looked at his phone and saw the
message from Gray. Shit! A double date!!

He paused, so tempted to just say no and spend the day
sorting out the boxes that were waiting to be unpacked.

**Look, I'm not sure I'm ready for a date let alone one at
your Sunday soiree event.** He typed back.

Ewan, you need to meet this girl! Gray typed back. Ewan
took a slug of his beer, the paperback lying in front of him
on the table.

I might have found my mystery girl; I don't think anyone else is going to be enough to match her. Ewan replied, as he picked up the paperback and opened to the first page.

Well maybe this is your dream girl, and she has a friend to die for!! Gray replied, he was hanging on to his trump card of the Jaguar Sports car.

Fine, I'll come over after my gym session. Ewan said, as the story started to pull him in.

Great, see you at noon.

Ewan didn't bother to reply as he was already half-way down the first page. He eventually closed the book at 2.30am in the morning. Climbing the stairs, he jumped into bed, determined to do some research in the morning if his internet was running by then. He owed it Gray to go through with this blind date but after that if CL Bennett turned out to be his Cara then there was only one thing on his mind, finding her and asking her out on a proper date.

CHAPTER 11

Sunday morning dawned with a brightness and lightness that caused flutters in Tania's stomach. She was going on a date with a guy who was not just adorable but could cook as well. Gray was up early preparing for the afternoon, the steaks were marinating, and the rest of the meat was defrosting ready for the BBQ. All he had to do later was shower, dress and prepare himself for Tania. The alarm woke Ewan and he struggled out of bed to the shower so that he had time to ride over for his personal training session, Matt hated lateness so he only had time for a coffee before setting off. His internet had still been off so any further investigation of author CL Bennett would have to wait for another day. Matt worked his butt off so by the end of the hour Ewan couldn't wait to get home for another shower.

It was Mansell that woke Cara with a lick and a bark in her ear, he wanted to go out. She stared blearily at the alarm clock which said ten, so she knew she had enough time for a coffee before Tania arrived. Opening her laptop on the table she stared at the last page that she'd written, still unsure of the ending that would suit the best. Should it be at the glitz and glamour of the track? or was that too predictable? What about in a supermarket or on a bus? She was just buttering her slice of toast when Tania burst through the door, bags in hand and her usually tidy hair in a messy bun. "Toast?" Cara asked, getting up from her blank screen and putting some more slices of bread in the toaster and a mug under the coffee pot.

"Yes, and yes" Tania replied, dropping her bags and sitting

down. The power went off in the flat just before I got in the shower, that's why I'm early as I'll need to use yours.

"No problem," she replied, buttering the toast and putting the plate in front of her friend. Tania had seen the open laptop and was craning her neck to try and read the words on the screen. Cara closed it and laughed, "You know the rules, not until I'm finished."

"When will that be?" Tania asked, between mouthfuls of toast. "Soon, I'm just wondering whether the ending I wrote last night is the best one." "Maybe this afternoon's date will give you some inspiration?" "Mmmh, maybe."

While Cara dried her hair and scooped her curls into a ponytail, Tania flung open the wardrobe and started to rifle through the hangers. "I think you should wear this?" she said, pulling out the dress that Cara had worn to the book signing. "Not that one," Cara said, blushing so much that Tania realised and said, "Oh is this the dress you wore when you met Ewan?" "Yes," she replied. Tania hung it back up as Cara gazed at it longingly, wondering if she would ever meet him again. "Get me the poppy dress, it's a perfect Sunday afternoon dress and even in my rush I remembered to pick up my red handbag for you to borrow."

"What are you wearing?" Cara asked, as Tania pulled out her navy pencil skirt and white spot print top. "This, so long as I can borrow your blue handbag and those white sandals?" Cara nodded and smiled, feeling a slight nervous excitement in her stomach, more for her friend than her own date. This guy Gray had really dazzled Tania the previous evening and as both of them had been single for so long it would be good for one of them to be in a relationship.

Ewan climbed on his bike, he was nervous about this blind date, but he had at least had time to phone and leave a message to his new internet provider, asking when he'd be online. By getting over to the pub slightly early he knew Gray would be more than happy to let him do a little research on his computer before the afternoon date. However, the traffic conspired against him and he was soon sweating in his leather's that he'd be late. Everyone seemed to be heading into the countryside but as the weather was a perfect summer day, he couldn't really blame them. The car park was half full when he pulled in and parked his bike in the small yard directly behind the restaurant. He knew it would be safe there and not get knocked over or boxed in should he need to get away. Gray had good taste in women but Ewan knew that none would come close to Cara, especially if she did turn out to be CL Bennett.

"I thought you'd ducked out on me?" Gray said, opening the kitchen door and letting him in. "Is there any chance you could go and tell the band where to set up as I'm up to my ears in wrapping jacket potatoes, they need to be on the fire pit now but I'm running late.

"Sure, it will give me something to do before my blind date arrives with your date, "Ewan replied. "Look man, you won't regret it. This girl I have lined up is going to blow your mind."

"What's her name?" he replied.

"I can't remember, but she'd gorgeous." Gray said, turning away to hide the laugh erupting inside. He was almost certain that this girl was the one his friend was looking for, his lay-by liaison. Gray wrapped the last potatoes and then once they were on the fire, he left his sous chef in charge so that he had time to get changed. He'd sent the taxi half an hour ago and knew they would be here soon. Returning to the bar he heard the steady beat of a drummer as the band tuned up. The picnic benches and rugs were filling up outside and the bar was humming with conversation and drink orders.

"Any chance of a beer?" Ewan asked, "It's thirsty work being your lackey!" Pouring them both a pint, Gray walked around the bar and pressed one in his mate's hand. A couple close by had recognised Ewan and the chap was walking towards them.

"Looks like you've been spotted?" Gray said, stepping aside so that Ewan could shake hands and write a quick autograph on the napkin nearby for the man. "I hope you've found us a quiet spot outside as I don't need any more autograph hunters while I'm being your wing man."

"Of course, follow me as I need to just check on the food."

They both walked outside and Gray had a long look at the various grills that were on the go. Some people had already grabbed a burger or hot dog and were piling up their plates with the usual sauces and salads that were on offer. "We're at the table near the back," he motioned, whilst scanning the arriving cars for the taxi he was waiting for. He'd never been more excited in his life at potentially solving his mate's singledom. Ewan sat with his back to the rest of the revellers, feeling there was less chance of being spotted, Gray was opposite and in the perfect position to survey the crowds, band, food and of course the car park. Then he saw the taxi pull up and he took a deep breath, Ewan noticed this and smiled. It was strange to see his confidant mate looking so flustered.

"Go and grab us some drinks, and a bottle of rose for the girls." Gray asked.

"Sure." Ewan was glad of the chance to escape; he'd feel far more comfortable arriving back at the table when they were all seated. Or even better he could give them a glance out of the window of the pub and if his date looked awful, he could cut and run. Tania was the first to get out of the cab, smoothing her skirt down over her enviable curves as she spotting Gray immediately. Cara got out next and saw that Gray was alone, she wondered if a blind date had just been a ruse and she was now going to have to play gooseberry for the rest of the afternoon.

"Tania, you're looking stunning." Gray said, catching her hand and bringing it up to his lips. Tania smiled and replied, "You're looking good too." Her eyes running down his tight t-shirt and over his snug jeans. Cara stared across the crowded grounds, seeing all the happy couples and families at different tables and knowing that an afternoon of people watching was always good inspiration for a novel or two. She had her trusty iPad in the handbag so if she needed to disappear, she could find a quiet spot and write. "Cara, it's lovely to see you again and I can't wait for you to meet my friend. He's just gone to the bar so I hope Rose wine will be suitable for you both?"

"Thank you, that's very kind." Cara replied as she followed Gray who had placed his hand very protectively around Tania's waist. Tania looked over her shoulder and winked at Cara, who smiled back. He showed them to the table, sitting next to Tania and letting Cara take the seat opposite her friend.

Ewan waited for the drinks and stole a glance out of the

window, he saw Gray walking back to the table with his arm around the waist of a brunette, behind them walked a blond who from this distance looked good, her curly hair reminded him of Cara but these were more restrained in a pony tail. Gray was his friend, his best friend so he carefully loaded up the tray and weaved his way through the people in the bar and out to the table.

Gray saw him and stood up, suddenly worried that when Ewan clapped eyes on Cara, he'd be so surprised that potentially the bottle of wine and glasses would not stay steady on the tray.

"I'll just go and give Ewan a hand," he said, as out of the corner of his eye he saw Cara start at the name. She slowly turned her head but discovered that Gray was now blocking her view of his returning friend. "Tania, did he say his friend is called Ewan?" Cara gasped, still trying to see past Gray.

"Oh my god, do you think it might be your Ewan?" Tania replied, she was also craning her neck to try and see her friend's mystery date.

"Here, let me help you," Gray said, grabbing the neck of the bottle and the two wine glasses, leaving Ewan with just their bottles of beer on the tray. Slowly Gray turned to head back to the table, walking alongside his friend. Cara gasped and felt a blush burning up her cheeks because it was her Ewan. But would he be happy to see her?

79

CHAPTER 12

As Ewan got closer to the table, he had the sudden realisation that the blind date at the table was his Cara, how could this be happening. He blinked a couple of times whilst trying to stop his hands from shaking as they gripped the tray. He glanced across at Gray and mouthed "Is this real or am I dreaming?"

"It's real mate, I guess I struck lucky for you." Ewan just nodded and hoped his mouth hadn't gone into some drippy grin. At the table he put down the tray and Gray said "Cara, Tania can I introduce my best mate Ewan. You might recognise him if you're into bikes."

Tania stuck out her hand to shake his and she could feel the tension in his body, she hoped he was as happy about this meeting as her friend was.

"Hi, it's great to meet you, any chance of an autograph?" she giggled, hoping it would ease the palpable electricity that was buzzing in the air. Then it was like a slow motion shot on a tv show as Cara turned to look at him and their eyes locked, like the last time they saw each other.

Cara took a deep breath and said "Hey, Ewan it took you a while." She blushed as she said the line, hearing it in her mind and thinking that it sounded like a corny statement from a badly written soap opera. All she could think about was their last meeting, the hour of passion under the stars in a deserted lay-by. She felt his eyes drinking her in and all she wanted him to do was lift her up and carry her away, like Richard Gere in the film "An Officer and a Gentleman", in fact the song started playing in her mind.

Ewan sat down on the bench next to her as Gray passed around the drinks and took his place next to Tania. Cara and Ewan were aware that their respective friends were just staring at them across the table so they both picked up their drinks.

"Well, what a happy coincidence," Ewan muttered, wishing the ground would swallow him up. He needed time alone with her. She must have felt his discomfort as she slid her free hand across the bench seat and inched her hand beneath his. The feel of her skin was like a jolt to his system and he gave it a squeeze and felt her tremble.

"Shall we get some food?" Gray asked.

"Yes, please." Tania replied.

"Uh, we'll take a minute," Ewan said, hardly able to breath. This was his chance, but did he feel able to take it? Would she say yes or would polite friendship protocol prevent it. The band started their first number as Ewan took a breath and leaned in, his breath tickled the skin on her neck, and she leaned in closer. "I can't talk to you here, come with me somewhere private."

"Yes," she breathed, feeling his lips touch her cheek in a tender kiss that caught her off guard. Cara had never been reckless in her life but here she was abandoning her friend to ride off with a stranger she only knew from one night and a thousand press and magazine articles. They waited until Gray and Tania had walked away and then he stood up and held out his hand. She grasped it and stifling a giggle they ran across the grass and round the back of the pub. His motorbike was waiting and in just a few moments he'd opened a small, shed door and pulled out a helmet. "I think this should fit," he said, placing it on her head. She nodded and smiled, suddenly apprehensive about being on the back of a bike. He must have seen her shake as he reached for her hand and gave it a squeeze "I'll take care of you, trust me."

Cara waited for him to climb on and then gathering up her dress she climbed on behind him and instinctively wrapped her arms around his waist. She breathed in the smell of his leather jacket and the scent of Cool Waters and sighed. Ewan turned the key and the engine throbbed beneath them and with a quick glance around he took off through the car park, trying not to get distracted by the feel of Cara pressing against him. He knew just where to take her, and it wasn't too far away.

The sound of the bike engine made Gray and Tania turn around in time to see their friends departing backs as they left the car park. Gray looked at Tania and she did the same and they both started to laugh. "Looks like we've been abandoned." Gray said.

"I have never known Cara to do anything that reckless…well apart from the night they both originally met." Tania said, wondering how much Gray knew about that night.

"Yeah, Ewan's the same really. I've known him since we were at school and I always had to prompt him to make any sort of move." As the band started to play, Gray filled their plates and they walked back to the table.

With the countryside flashing past Cara waited until they pulled to a stop in a very familiar place, it was their lay-by. She carefully dismounted, aware that her thighs had been gripping the bike for the whole journey and her body was filled with nervous tension. Ewan untied her helmet and placed it with his to tie onto the bike. Then he pulled her close and for the first time since that night he felt totally at home. He reached his hand into her hair and pulled out the clasp that held her ponytail in, feeling her curls slipping through his fingers like they had the first time. His heart was pounding, and he knew she must feel it through their clothing. "Come with me," he whispered in her ear, sneaking another soft kiss onto the skin of her cheek. "Yes," she breathed, as he took her hand and led her along the path, then onto the grass as he found their spot.

Shrugging off his jacket he laid it on the ground and dropped onto it, Cara followed suit and he put his arm around her shoulders. "I want it to be like last time but different…" he paused, not sure how to say this without mentioning the L word. "I need you to know how I feel, I've been going crazy since that encounter, especially since I only knew your first name."

Cara turned to look into his eyes and melted, knowing exactly how he was feeling. She opened her mouth to say something but had no words to convey the way she felt. Last time had been pure passion but this time it was true love.

He captured her lips with his and they opened to explore, the feelings were thrilling yet familiar and within moments she had moved to straddle him. Every so often they paused and just looked into each other's eyes. But Ewan was determined that this time it was going to be different and during one of their pauses he spoke. "I want to do this properly, not out here where anyone could see us. I want to take my time, get to really know you." He blushed, feeling like he was in one of her romance novels. She climbed off him and this time reached out her hand, accepting without a word his idea.

They walked back to the bike and she reached into her handbag. "I just need to make a call and send a text," she said, "In case I forget later." She smiled at Ewan and saw his face light up. Pressing dial, she got through to her neighbour Lynn. "Can you pop in and let Mansell out this evening, make sure he has food and water and then again first thing tomorrow?"

"Sure, is everything all right?"

"Absolutely and thank you."

Then she sent a quick text to Tania. **I'm fine, in fact I'm more than fine. Sorry I skipped out on the date, but I'll fill you in tomorrow. Don't do anything I wouldn't do!! X**

With her phone on silence she nodded.

"So, who is Mansell?" Ewan asked.

"He's my dog, I named him after the formula one driver. He was my Dad's favourite."

"You're a fan of motorsport then?"

"You could say that."

He gave her the helmet and she put it on and then she was back behind him, holding on and wondering where they were going this time. Ewan drove carefully along the lanes that led to his new house and when they pulled in, he hopped off the bike and as she climbed off he picked her up into his arms and carried her to the front door. He had to put her down to get the key into the lock and then ushered her inside. Taking her hand, she followed as they went up the staircase and into his bedroom. All that was inside was a king size bed and the boxes and suitcases waiting for the rest of his furniture to arrive.

"I'm sorry it's a mess, I've only just moved in." Ewan said, blushing as he watched her look around. "Well, at least you have a bed," she replied, walking towards it. Her whole body was tingling with pent up desire. She turned to look at him and he didn't need any other words of invitation. He turned her away from him and found the zip on her dress, pulling it down and sighing as he saw the white lace underwear beneath. As she turned back to face him her fingers grabbed the hem of his t-shirt and pulled it upwards to reveal the skin she had missed. Running her hands over the firm muscles and then to his shoulders, he coiled his around her waist until they were skin to skin once more. Her lips opened to his as they kissed for what seemed like an eternity before he pushed her back onto the soft sheets of the bed. He pulled off his jeans and then stared at her, drinking in every curve and swell of her body. Cara felt her skin turn pink under his gaze and held open her arms so that he would fill them once more. But instead he knelt beside her letting his lips start at hers before then travelling down her neck, over her collar bone and his fingers eased down the straps of her bra.

Her nipples sprung into life beneath his fingers and then his tongue as he licked and sucked and nipped at them, while he felt her hands running through his hair. Cara sighed and held him there, this moment was like all her birthdays had come together. Then she felt his tongue move lower, over

85

her stomach and then his fingers brushed over the lace of her panties. Her clit was already tingling, and she moaned as he took a moment to pause and look up at her. "Please keep going," she cried, and he nodded as he slowly hooked his fingers into the elastic, and she arched up so that he could pull them off. She watched as they fell onto the floor and his finger gently stroked reverently up her thighs and delved into her folds.

Cara closed her eyes, her hands clenched around the sheets and her breathing rate increased as his tongue took over. She remembered how good he had been in the lay-by but this time it was better as he took more time, gently sucking and licking at her clit as she mewled her response and urged him back as he seemed to bring her to the peak of her orgasm and then leave her hanging there as his tongue traced patterns onto her inner thighs. When she came close for the third time she pushed her hips up and clamped his head with her thighs, without words he knew she wanted the release so he doubled his pace and felt her shudder and drown his tongue in her juice. Ewan knew he wouldn't last if he let her suck him, so he shrugged off his boxer's and reached over to his bedside cabinet. At least he had unpacked some things!

She gazed at him as he leaned over and gently let her lips plant kisses on the nearest part of his body. He looked in wonder at her as she lay waiting for him, she was perfect, and he hoped that she was his now. He knew he didn't want anyone else in his life. Reading her novel had given him a small insight into the sort of person she was, and he just yearned to know more and more and let himself fall deeper and deeper in love with her. He knelt reverently between her open thighs and glanced a small nod of consent from her. Then he nudged inside her, feeling the grip around him and he drew in a breath. He didn't want to explode just yet, he wanted to make her come even more. He gently eased in and out, slowly at first so that he had time between each stroke to kiss her upturned lips.

Cara wanted to take control and as he was tight inside her she held him close and he took the hint and they rolled together so that she was on top. Her hair cascaded over her shoulders, her nipples were rosy, and he held her hips and slid his hands up and down her slender curves. She started off slowly, rocking back and forth and revelling in the feel of him. She let her hands run up and down his chest and as the need inside her built to a crescendo at the same point as he did. He felt her still as he did and then she fell upon him, hot and beautiful in his arms. Ewan paused, he had been trying not to say it but he knew that he could no longer stay silent. "Cara, I love you." She looked straight into his eyes and replied, "I love you."

EPILOGUE

Cara padded across the wooden floorboards, she pulled the thin curtains apart and gazed out onto the clean white sand and the turquoise sea. It had been a mere month before Ewan had dropped to the floor when they had been dining at Gray's pub to celebrate their first month anniversary. Gray must have been in on it as he produced a magnum of champagne and four glasses. Tania had squealed so loudly from her seat next to Cara and leaned in to kiss her face as soon as Ewan had finished. "I can't believe this is all happening, it's like living in the best romance novel ever!" Tania had whispered, before she stared up at Gray as he dropped a kiss on her upturned lips.

Ewan had promptly booked the chapel and in a whirlwind Tania had helped her shop for the perfect dress. She glanced over her shoulder to see its now crumpled form on the small sofa of their suite. Ewan's Mum had turned out to be Jean from the book signing as she recalled the first time he had taken her over to meet her. Cara had met slightly more resistance from her parents who felt they should warn their daughter about the perils of dating a sports star. It hadn't helped that they were the paparazzi's favourite new couple and were frequently followed everywhere. That was both a blessing and a curse, the blessing being that she had now gone from averagely successful author to Time's Bestseller overnight.

The sea breeze caught the slight hint of the salt and carried it through into the room, along with a cooling breeze that was welcome after the heat of last night. She looked across to see Ewan still sprawled on the bed, his dark hair ruffled on the pillow and a contented smile on his face. She looked back out of the window, watching a young girl on the beach doing what looked like yoga. A man's form bobbed up in the ocean and seemed to tread water as he watched the girl. Cara smiled, yes, a beach romance would be perfect to get started on whilst she was on honeymoon. She was so caught up in watching this first look moment that she didn't hear Ewan wake and creep out of bed, until his arms circled her waist, and his lips nuzzled her neck with sweet kisses.

"Morning Mrs Michaels," he said, as she turned around and into his embrace. "Morning Mr Michaels" she replied. Thrilled to be both hearing and saying the words that she thought only ever happened in a romance novel. Now she was living in hers.

THE END

ABOUT THE AUTHOR

Expect the unexpected with Audrina's 'Where words and Music collide'. You may not get the traditional Happy Ever After Ending you were expecting!

Website: http://audrinalane.co.uk/

Find all of Audrina's novels on Amazon and most are enrolled in Kindle Unlimited:

https://www.amazon.co.uk/Audrina-Lane/e/B00E263F96/ref=ntt_dp_epwbk_0

https://www.amazon.com/Audrina-Lane/e/B00E263F96/ref=ntt_dp_epwbk_0

Audrina lives in Herefordshire with her partner Steve and her 2 black Labrador dogs.

She is the author of the fabulous "Heart Trilogy Series" made up of the novels "Where did your Heart go?" "Un-break my Heart" and "Closer to the Heart" She has also completed the Bloodstained Heart Trilogy. These are connected to The Heart Trilogy series in that they feature the full story of Felicity.

She writes in partnership with Rita Ames on the 'Need for Speed' Racing series. These are romances set at various different motor racing venues, with the first book '24Hrs to Love' set at Le Mans.

When not writing Audrina enjoys watching Formula 1, and loves the Star Wars films with a passion. She listens to 80's music and has been a big fan of George Michael and Wham! since her teenage years. Music is so integral to her life that most of her book titles are also the titles of songs she likes and that have a connection to the storyline.

OTHER BOOKS BY AUDRINA LANE

The Heart Trilogy

Where did your Heart go?

Unbreak my Heart

Closer to the Heart

The Bloodstained Heart Trilogy

Bloodstained Heart, Part 1 – Passion

Bloodstained Heart, Part 2 – Revenge

Bloodstained Heart, Part 3 – Redemption

Need for Speed Trilogy with Rita Ames

24Hrs to Love

Standalone

A Whiter shade of Pale – Poetry & Short stories

Bonfire Heart

Victory 75 – Short story compilation with other authors.

SOCIAL MEDIA

Find Audrina on Social Media, including Facebook, Twitter, Instagram and YouTube:

Instagram: https://www.instagram.com/audrinalane/

YouTube:
https://www.youtube.com/channel/UC3ZISOU53eaoLHOCNJNg gCA?view_as=subscriber

Twitter: https://twitter.com/AudrinaLane

Facebook: https://www.facebook.com/audrina.lane

Audrina's Place: https://www.facebook.com/AudrinasPlace/

24Hrs Facebook Page:
https://www.facebook.com/RaceRomance/

Can I Ask A Favour?

If you enjoyed this book, found it useful or otherwise then I'd really appreciate it if you would post a short review on Amazon. I do read all the reviews personally so that I can continually write what people are wanting.

If you'd like to leave a review, then please visit the link below:

Thanks for your support!

Audrina Lane

Drive By: An Electric Eclectic Novel eBook: Lane, Audrina: Amazon.co.uk: Kindle Store

Drive By: An Electric Eclectic Novel - Kindle edition by Lane, Audrina. Literature & Fiction Kindle eBooks @ Amazon.com.

Printed in Great Britain
by Amazon